Meili and Wenling

Written by;
Barbara Kristof
and
Rosemary Woods

Illustrated by Barbara Kelley

PAGE PUBLISHING, INC.
Conneaut Lake, PA

First originally published by Page Publishing 2021

ISBN 978-1-6624-4395-4 (pbk)
ISBN 978-1-6624-4396-1 (digital)

Printed in the United States of America

Dedication

To all our panda friends and the children who love them

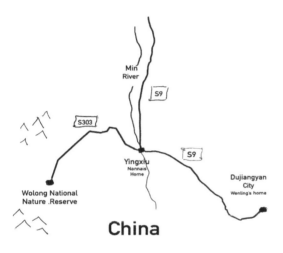

Wolong National Nature Reserve

Yingxiu *(grandmother's house)*

Dujiangyan City *(Wenling's house)*

Since this story takes place in China, near the Wolong National Nature Reserve, the names may be unfamiliar to you. Here are the names of the people in the story and how you say them.

Năinai	(Nay-nuh)	Heng	(hang)
Wenling	(wun-LEENG)	Jianyu	(Jee-on-you)
Meili	(may-lee)	Zhangwei	(Jahng-way)
Liling	(LEE-ling)	Zhiming	(Jee-ming)
Chunhua	(chun-HWA)	Weixin	(Way-sin)

Wenling opened her eyes and looked around. For a moment, she had no idea where she was. But then she saw the familiar photo of her mother as a young girl—and she remembered that she was at Nǎinai's house. She smiled—being with her grandmother always made her happy.

She jumped out of bed and ran toward the kitchen. She could hear her grandmother making breakfast.

"Good morning, Năinai," she cried as she stretched her arms wide and reached up to wrap them around the thighs of her grandmother's long legs. "Something smells good! And I am starving!"

Her grandmother laughed, turned around, and picked her up.

"Oh my goodness!" she cried as she locked her in her special grandmother hug.

"You are such a big girl! You've gotten so big since you turned five I can hardly pick you up!

Do you remember what's happening today? And tomorrow?" Năinai asked.

"*Yes*!" Wenling cried happily, her eyes shining. "Mom and Dad are coming, and tomorrow we are all going to see the pandas!"

Năinai lived close to the Wolong National Nature Reserve, home to many giant pandas. A trip to see the pandas was Wenling's birthday present from her mom and dad.

"Are you excited?" Năinai asked as she smiled at Wenling.

"*Yes!*" Wenling cried again as her grandmother set her down. "I can't wait to see the pandas. I hope there are some babies."

"Oh, I'm quite sure there are," her grandmother said. "Now let's have some breakfast, and then I have a surprise for you. A late birthday present!"

"Oh, what is it?" Wenling asked.

"Well, I can't tell you until you have finished your breakfast. Then we'll look at it together."

In addition to breakfast porridge, Năinai had prepared two of Wenling's favorites: shrimp dumplings and savory red bean buns. They sat together for an hour, enjoying the delicious food, sipping Năinai's amazing tea, and talking about all the exciting things going on in Wenling's life.

After everything in the kitchen was put away, Nǎinai told Wenling to go to their favorite chair and close her eyes. When she opened them, Nǎinai was standing in front of her, smiling and holding a package with a big bow on the top.

Wenling was *very* happy when she saw what was inside the package: it was a beautiful picture of a panda bear—looking straight at her and happily munching bamboo. "Oh, Nǎinai!" Wenling cried. "It's a book about the pandas!"

Nǎinai loved the giant pandas and wanted her granddaughter to learn about them. Many years ago, she herself had spent some time at the Wolong National Nature Reserve, so she knew exactly what kind of book to order for her granddaughter. She had chosen a book with beautiful photos of panda bears but also many interesting facts about them—what they eat, how they play, how much they sleep.

The two of them sat in the chair together for two hours, Năinai reading aloud and Wenling listening carefully and oohing and aahing over the amazing photos.

When they reached the end of the book, Wenling knew much, much more about panda bears—and she was more excited than ever about going to see them.

By the time her mom and dad arrived from Dujiangyan (Doo-jyahng-yahn) City, Wenling was jumping up and down with excitement and could hardly wait to show them her new book. They ate lunch, and then she sat down with her parents and looked through the book again. She shared with them everything she had learned from Năinai.

They were very impressed with how much Wenling already knew about pandas. Her excitement was contagious, and her mom and dad admitted that they, too, were eager to meet some pandas.

Wenling knew they were going to get an early start the next morning, so she didn't have to be told twice to go to bed when it was bedtime. As she lay her head on the pillow, she knew that tomorrow was going to be a very special day.

By eleven o'clock the next morning, they had arrived. As they walked together to the entrance of the Reserve, they could see the welcoming stone building, tall trees, and bright green plants of the Wolong National Nature Reserve—just like she had seen in the book!

Wenling didn't think she had ever been so happy as she waited her turn to go in.

Finally, they gave the keeper their tickets, walked through the gate, and began their tour of the panda homes.

They stopped at many stations along the tour, and in each one, Wenling saw pandas of all sizes—sitting together and eating bamboo, playing together, climbing trees.

In one station, Wenling was sure she saw two young panda bears dancing! And in another, she watched four little panda bears, sitting side by side, topple over like dominoes!

Around noon, she stopped to watch a mother and baby panda playing. The baby was crawling onto her mom's shoulders and then falling to the ground, gently helped by her mother. The baby was a bundle of energy—standing, crawling, constantly jumping up and down.

In the middle of trying to eat a bamboo leaf, the baby panda stopped, and very slowly, turned her head around. She stared directly at Wenling. They seemed to be held together like magnets—Wenling couldn't take her eyes away—and the little panda just kept looking straight at her.

Wenling's mother watched her daughter and the baby panda as they looked at each other, and she was happy that she had learned the baby panda's name. She whispered it to Wenling.

"Meili," Wenling said softly. "What a pretty name."

Meili's mother, Zhiming, also noticed that her baby was looking at the human girl. She got up very slowly, put her arms around her daughter—and they both stood there for a few more minutes: a panda family and a human family, looking at each other—the mothers with caution, the daughters with curiosity and fascination.

Finally, Zhiming turned away, put Meili on her back, and slowly walked toward their cave.

Meili kept looking at Wenling—and just before she entered the cave with her mother, Zhiming, she lifted a tiny paw in Wenling's direction, as though she was saying goodbye. Wenling waved back, smiling from ear to ear. In her heart, she knew that she had made a new friend—and that she would see Meili again. Zhiming looked back toward Wenling at the last moment—and she seemed to have something like a smile on her face. Maybe she felt the same way Wenling's mother did—happy that her daughter had just made a new friend.

When it was time to leave, Wenling and her family said goodbye to the pandas and returned to Năinai's house. On the way home, Wenling chattered on and on about her new friend. She told her family that she *knew* she would come back to see Meili again.

Wenling finally fell asleep with her head in her grandmother's lap. When they got home, her father lifted her out of the car and carried her inside. Her parents helped her get into her nightclothes.

As she was getting into her bed, she got the biggest surprise of the day: lying quietly on her pillow, looking at her with bright, brown eyes, was a baby panda!

She squealed with delight, jumped into bed, and lay down beside the panda bear.

"Who are you? Where did you come from?" she asked the panda bear.

No one else could hear the answer, but Wenling clearly heard, "I am Meili, and I have come to be your friend."

There was so much Wenling wanted to know: Did Meili come from Wolong? How did she get to Wenling's house? What was it like living in a giant panda reserve? What does bamboo taste like? And Meili answered all her questions, in a voice so soft and quiet that only Wenling could hear it.

Wenling fell asleep in the middle of their conversation.

When Wenling woke up the next morning, she was very happy to see that Meili was still there. In fact, she was already awake—and seemed to be waiting for Wenling to wake up so they could start the day.

She showed her mom and dad the bear and told them her name: Meili. Though they both seemed surprised that a panda had come to their house, they were very happy to meet Wenling's new friend.

From that day forward, Wenling and Meili were like two peas in a pod: they ate together, played together, and slept together.

When Wenling started school, she had to leave Meili at home, but in the evening, she taught Meili everything she had learned at school. And so Meili also learned to read, add and subtract numbers, and sing songs.

Though Wenling barely noticed it, she was changing now that Meili was her friend. Shortly after the visit to Wolong, Wenling was playing with her good friend Chunhua. Chunhua wanted to play checkers, and Wenling wanted to play with her new paper dolls. Wenling whispered to Meili that sometimes Chunhua made her *so* angry. Meili just looked at Wenling. And a thought popped into Wenling's head: Actually, Chunhua is a very nice girl. She comes over whenever I want her to, and when I tell her a secret, she always keeps it to herself. She's a very good friend.

Wenling turned to her friend Chunhua and said, "You know what? That's a good idea. Let's play checkers." And they did. And after they had played for a while, Chunhua said, "Now let's play with your new paper dolls."

From then on, Wenling remembered that when you have a friend, you don't always get your way. Sometimes you have to let your friends do what makes them happy. She understood now that when you make sure your friend is happy, it somehow comes back to you and makes you happy too.

The next day, Wenling was feeling lazy. Her mom had asked her to pick up her toys and put them away—but she just didn't feel like it. She was reading her favorite book when she looked over at Meili. Meili didn't actually *say* anything—but a thought popped into Wenling's head. "Remember that great breakfast Mom cooked this morning? She's probably pretty tired, and she might feel *really* good if she came in and saw that all the toys were put away."

Wenling *did* remember that delicious breakfast, so she jumped up and quickly put everything in its place. The remarkable thing was: it hardly took her any time at all. She knew exactly where everything belonged. And it made her feel good to know that all her toys were in their proper places. She thought maybe the toys liked that too.

When her mother came in, she looked in amazement at the neat room before her with everything in its place. She picked Wenling up and gave her a big hug.

"Thank you, Wenling," she said. "You are a blessing to me."

It made Wenling very happy. She looked at Meili, who just looked back at her with her dark brown eyes—and her funny little smile.

Later that week, Wenling was lying on the floor in her bedroom, painting a picture. She accidentally spilled some of the paint on the floor, and it made a big mess. She was afraid to tell her mom and dad—she didn't want them to be angry with her. So she was looking around, trying to find something to cover up the mess.

Meili was sitting beside her, just looking at her with those eyes of hers! A thought popped into Wenling's head, and she said to herself, "I'd better tell them. They'll find it anyway, and not telling them is no different from telling a lie." She ran into the kitchen where they were drinking tea and reading the newspaper, and she told them that she was sorry but that she had accidentally spilled some paint on the floor. Her dad got up, reached into the cabinet to grab a rag and something in a spray can—and went with her into her bedroom. Together, while her dad talked to her about the picture she was painting, they cleaned the spot—and you couldn't even see where the paint had been.

Her dad said, "Thank you for telling me, Wenling. If you had let the paint dry on the floor, it would have been much harder to get off." He gave her a little kiss on the cheek and went back to his newspaper.

Wenling looked at Meili. She was slowly beginning to suspect that Meili was putting thoughts into her head—thoughts that helped her know how to do the right thing. It was like having your own guardian angel!

Over the next weeks, months, and years, Meili never let her down. When Wenling wasn't sure what to do, she would look at her friend—and somehow, the right thought would just pop into her head.

She found, over time, that those thoughts were showing up even when Meili was not in the same room. She wasn't sure what to make of that.

Meili could have told her that the good thoughts had always been there. Meili was just helping her find them.

Wenling loved going to school. She got to do all her favorite things—read, color, learn about numbers—and spend time with her friends. But in the fifth grade, there was a problem. There was one boy—Heng—who always made life hard for everyone else. He spoke too loudly, pushed people around, and always had to be at the first of the line. One day, he shoved Wenling's friend Jianyu—and Jianyu fell. Wenling wasn't sure what to do when suddenly a thought popped into her head: "Heng is a bully. If I don't stand up to him now and don't speak up for Jianyu, tomorrow, it might be Chunhua or someone else I care about. I must be brave."

Wenling turned back around, rapped Heng on the shoulder, and said, "Heng, didn't you notice that you knocked Jianyu down? You need to help him up and tell him you're sorry." Heng was stunned that someone had actually stood up to him—and a girl at that. He didn't help Jianyu up, but he did mumble "Sorry" as he plopped down in his seat.

He continued to be a bully, but Wenling noticed that the other children in the class didn't let him push them around so much. She hoped that with time, Heng would learn what she had learned from Meili—that whatever you put into the world comes back to you.

Wenling and her parents went back to Wolong as often as she could talk them into it. On every special occasion, like her birthday, she always wanted to go and see the pandas. And whenever they went, she would take Meili with her. They would stand for hours in front of the station where Zhiming and Meili lived. Wenling had no doubt that *her* Meili was somehow communicating with the two bears.

Through the years, as Wenling changed from a little girl to a teenager and eventually a young woman, she became very busy, and she spent less and less time with Meili. But Meili was always there: watching, caring, and listening to Wenling's problems that she didn't share with anyone else and, more than once, popping into her head to help her remember to do the right thing.

When Wenling left her home to study at the university, Meili went with her. She spent her days in a comfortable spot on the bookshelf—and her nights sleeping soundly on Wenling's pillow. She experienced through Wenling both the happiness and the hard work of being a student.

One day, Wenling was about to go to the library and thought to herself, *Why am I working so hard? I've studied enough for that test tomorrow. Maybe I'll just blow it off and take in a movie.*

She glanced up toward the shelf where Meili was sitting. And then a thought popped into her head: "That test tomorrow is very important. It might make a difference in whether I get an 85 or a 95. And *that* might make a difference in whether I get that internship at Wolong."

She looked again at Meili, sitting innocently on the shelf, pretending that she wasn't still, after all these years, sending thoughts into her head!

She sighed, and she finished packing her things for the library. Before she left, she walked over to the shelf, took Meili down, and gave her a big hug. As always, holding her bear made her feel calm and confident. As she placed Meili back on the shelf, she said to her, "Meili, you are a blessing to me."

She took the test, and she made an excellent grade: 100! At the end of the semester, she was thrilled to learn that she had, indeed, won the internship for the summer at the Wolong National Nature Reserve. She had been so happy to tell Năinai that she was going to work with the giant pandas. Deep down inside, she was pretty sure that Meili had helped her get that internship. There wasn't much doubt that Meili, too, wanted her to go to Wolong.

In the course of her time at the university, Wenling met a very nice young man, Zhangwei. They became good friends as they studied science and worked on projects together—and when they finished their studies, they got married—and both got jobs doing research at the Wolong National Nature Reserve. It was a dream come true for Wenling and Meili. It was, after all, something the two of them had often discussed as they lay in her bed at night.

On Wenling's twenty-fifth birthday, her daughter Liling was born. And five years later, on both their birthdays, they celebrated by having a picnic with their panda friends, Meili and Zhiming. Zhiming was very old by this time—and Meili had grown into a pretty big panda. She was, in fact, a mom herself. Her little panda was a boy and was named Weixin. Wenling couldn't help but notice that Liling seemed very interested in getting to know him!

When they went home from the picnic and Liling went into her bedroom to go to bed, she found a little panda lying on the pillow where she was about to put her head. She squealed with delight, grabbed the panda, and ran into the kitchen to show it to her mom and dad.

"Look! This panda bear has come to stay with me. His name is Weixin, just like the bear we met today! And he wants to be my friend."

Wenling hugged the panda and welcomed him into the family. As she watched her daughter going back to her room, carrying the little panda bear, Wenling was filled with love for her—and with gratitude that the friendship between the panda family and her human family that had begun so many years ago was still going on.

She couldn't wait to find out what Liling would learn from Weixin.

A few days later, on a quiet afternoon, Wenling sat down with Meili and Weixin. As the three of them sat together, the memories of all the things that had happened since her fifth birthday came into Wenling's mind, from that first visit to the Wolong National Nature Reserve, to all the days that followed: the playtimes, the songs and games, the lessons learned. And as she let those memories flow through her, and she told Weixin about some of the things she and Meili had done together, tears of joy flowed down her cheeks.

Wenling felt blessed that Meili and Zhiming and Weixin—and all the amazing pandas were such a big part of her life. She had no doubt that her heart had grown much bigger because of them.

She said a quiet "thank-you" to Nǎinai, whose panda book started it all.

Things you might want to know about Wenling's stuffed bear, Meili:

Her story is based on the life and adventures of an actual stuffed panda, Molly, who came into Barbara's life through her daughter, Elisabeth, thirty-eight years ago and still sits comfortably on a shelf in Elisabeth's room. Molly was made in Germany and has traveled from Germany to Texas to Colorado and back to Texas, where she lives at this time.

Some fun facts you might want to know about the real Meili—and other pandas: https://www.wwf.org.uk/learn/fascinating-facts/pandas.

- Their black-and-white coloring gives them good camouflage in their environment.
- Their eyes are different from those of other bears. Pandas have vertical slits for pupils.
- The cubs are kept with their mothers 100 percent of the time for the first month of their life. They are very small and need the warmth and protection of their mothers.
- They are very courageous—and adventuresome. At five months, they are already climbing and falling all over the place. They usually start learning to climb by climbing on their mothers.

- They have an extended wristbone that they use like a thumb to help them grip food.

- They spend ten to sixteen hours a day feeding, mainly on bamboo.

- They need at least two different bamboo species to avoid starvation.

- Pandas typically lead a solitary life. They are excellent tree climbers, but they spend most of their time feeding. They can eat for fourteen hours a day, mainly bamboo, which is 99 percent of their diet (though they sometimes eat eggs or small animals too).

If you and your family would like to adopt a panda and help the World Wildlife Foundation (WWF), go to https://gifts.worldwildlife.org/gift-center/gifts/species-adoptions/panda.aspx.

About the Authors

The creation of *Meili and Wenling* is a team effort by Rosemary Woods, Barbara Kristof, and Barbara Kelley. Rosemary, from whose brain the story of Meili came, is a retired social worker living in San Antonio, Texas. She shared her idea with her sister, Barbara (Kristof), who took on the task of writing the story. Their friend Barbara Kelley created the illustrations that brought it all to life. Barbara is an artist and photographer whose San Antonio-based company, Edges of Art, does many variations of art, including computer, watercolor, oils, and cutouts. Barbara Kristof is a former editor and teacher who has lived in Austin, Texas, off and on for over forty years. During that time, she was an editor of foreign language textbooks and taught both the German language and English as a second language. Her residency in Austin was interrupted by a nine-year stay in Germany, where her daughter Elisabeth was born—and where Elisabeth's panda bear, Molly, on whom Meili's story is based, came into their lives. Barbara currently lives with Elisabeth and Molly in Austin and still does private tutoring in both German and English.

What I have learned about pandas

What I have learned about pandas

What I have learned about pandas

What I have learned about pandas

CPSIA information can be obtained
at www.ICGtesting.com
Printed in the USA
LVHW070746021121
702225LV00009B/260

9 781662 443954